Originally published as *Sammie in de winter* in Belgium and the Netherlands by Clavis Uitgeverij, 2017
English translation from the Dutch by Clavis Publishing Inc., New York

Visit us on the Web at www.clavis-publishing.com.

Sammy in the Winter written and illustrated by Anita Bijsterbosch

ISBN 978-1-60537-417-8

This book was printed in October 2019 at Wai Man Book Binding (China) Ltd.
Flat A, 9/F., Phase 1, Kwun Tong Industrial Centre, 472-484 Kwun Tong Road, Kwun Tong, Kowloon, H.K.

First Edition
10 9 8 7 6 5 4 3 2 1

SAMMY
in the Winter

Anita Bijsterbosch

Clavis

NEW YORK

"Yippee, it's snowing!" Sammy calls.
He runs toward the window
in his pajamas and slippers.
"Look, Hob," he says to his friend.
"Let's go play outside!"

Now Sammy and Hob are ready
to play outside.
Sammy pulls his sled up a high hill.
The snow cracks underneath his feet.
Crack . . . crack . . .
"Hold on tight, Hob!"

Sammy puts on his skates
to go on the ice.
He takes a step and . . . whoa!
The ice is very slippery.
Luckily Sammy can laugh about it.

Then Sammy has an idea.
He brings a chair to the ice.
It makes skating much easier.
And Hob gets a ride, too!

Time to ski!
Sammy heads down the hill.
Hob watches Sammy go.

Now Sammy makes some snowballs.
He tosses them into a little mound of snow.
"Watch out, Hob," Sammy calls.
The mound is getting big!

Then Sammy rolls a big
snowball. He places it
on top of the mound of snow.
Can you guess what Sammy is making?

Sammy is making a snowman!
"Here, Snowman, you can have
my hat and scarf. I don't want you
to get cold," Sammy says.